Battle for the Knotty List

Michael G. Lewis

Illustrated by Stan Jaskiel

PELICAN PUBLISHING COMPANY

GRETNA 2016

The word "Pelican" and the depiction of a pelican are trademarks of Pelican Publishing Company, Inc., and are registered in the U.S. Patent and Trademark Office.

ISBN 9781455621330
E-book ISBN 9781455621347

Printed in Malaysia

Published by Pelican Publishing Company, Inc.
1000 Burmaster Street, Gretna, Louisiana 70053

To Charles Schulz and the "Peanuts" gang for kick-starting my love
of reading and cartoons.

And, especially, to Linus, for conveying in his quiet wisdom the
true meaning of Christmas.
—Michael Lewis

To Judy, who always believed this would be possible.
—Stan Jaskiel

Me name is Cap'n McNasty,
An' I did what pirates do.
When I stole that little elf,
And didn't think it through.

Put him under lock and key,
But didn't have a plan.
On what we were supposed to do,
With that little man.

Had to have me pirate crew
Watch him night and day.
'Twas a mistake sure it was,
He had a lot to say!

He told them all of Santa,
how he'd come again,
with magic reindeer flyin'
and all those little men!

He told them of the toy shop,
the beautiful smell o' wood.
And all those lovely toys they
made for children who were good.

"Before we place them in the sack,
We bounce every ball.
And pogo sticks must be raced
down the toy shop hall."

When he told of tastin' pies,
and cookies that they'd check.
Billy Blue Eyes drooled so much
We had to swab the deck!

That crew was done with stealin',
Aye, they wuz done with me!
Me alone against them all,
In a mutiny!

Fought I did with everything
even mop and pail!
And several pirates ended up
Tangled in the sail!

We wuz fightin' long and hard,
When Danny the Dreg,
That sneaky li'l scallywag,
Put termites on me leg!

Captured Poutin' Pam, I did!
Held 'er o'er the sea!
"Victory is mine!" I said.
"The ship belongs to me!"

Suddenly it went pitch dark,
Fillin' me with dread.
'Twas that little elf who put
A bucket on me head!

They stuck me in a small skiff,
Pointed me toward land,
And shoved a single wood oar
In me one good hand!

Fought off sharks and stormy seas,
all that dreadful night,
And washed up on an island
nary a soul in sight!

It was dark and I was cold,
soaked right to the bone.
A cap'n now without a ship,
stranded all alone!

Spied a house upon a bluff,
A fire burnin' warm.
Knew it was me only hope,
To survive the storm.

Pushed and pulled at the door,
Finally fallin' in.
Gaze I did upon a beauty,
With whiskers on her chin!

On her stunnin' face, I swear,
Was a black eye patch.
When I spied her wooden leg,
I knew I found me match.

I said I was a captain
lookin' fer a mate.
With a twinkle in me eye,
I asked her fer a date.

That was many years ago,
I'm done bein' bad.
Got me a whole new crew now,
That call me "Cap'n Dad"!

Those other
pirates made it,
To that
Northern Pole.
Aboard me ship
the *Knotty List*,
The last thing
they ever stole.

Their days are filled
with singin',
as they work away,
makin' sure there's
lots of toys
for kids on
Christmas Day.

Never thought I'd see me kin,
celebrate the season.
An' me nasty, bad 'ol days,
Surely was the reason.

But 'twas a Christmas miracle
When we found across our floor,
piles and piles of lovely gifts,
and sweets by the score!

I knew St. Nick forgave me,
for all that I had done.
'Cuz under that tree, was me name
on a new pop gun!